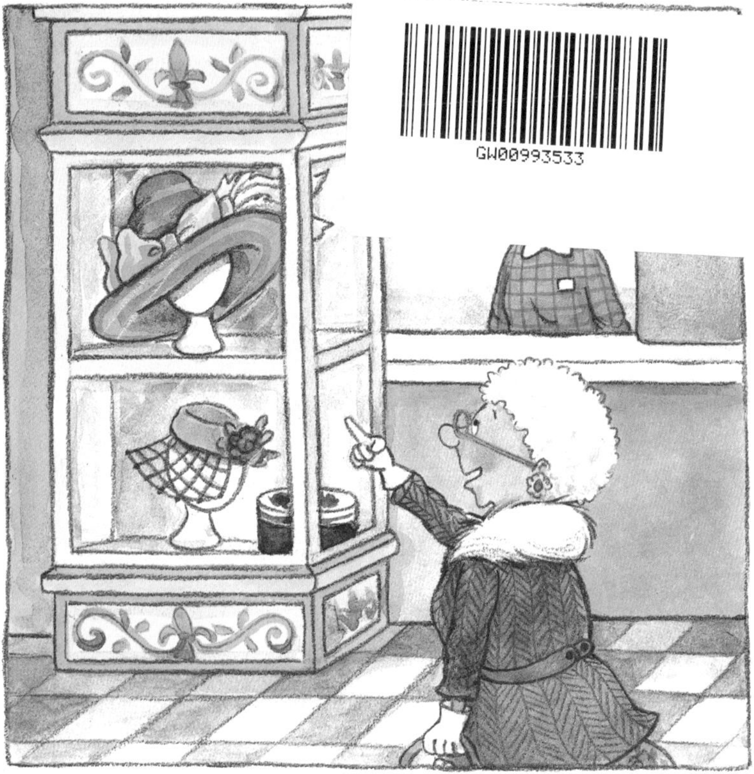

That hat.

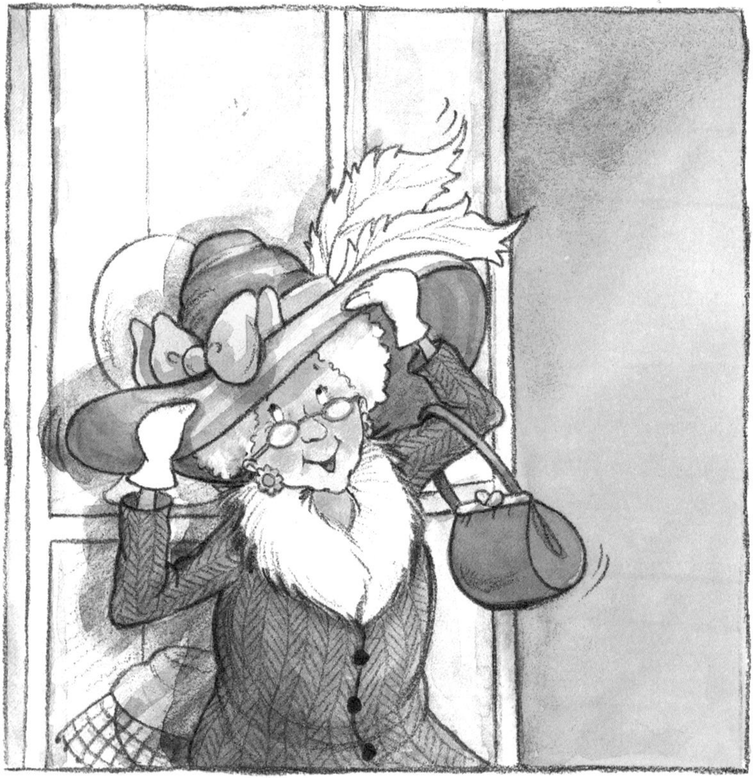

My pretty hat.

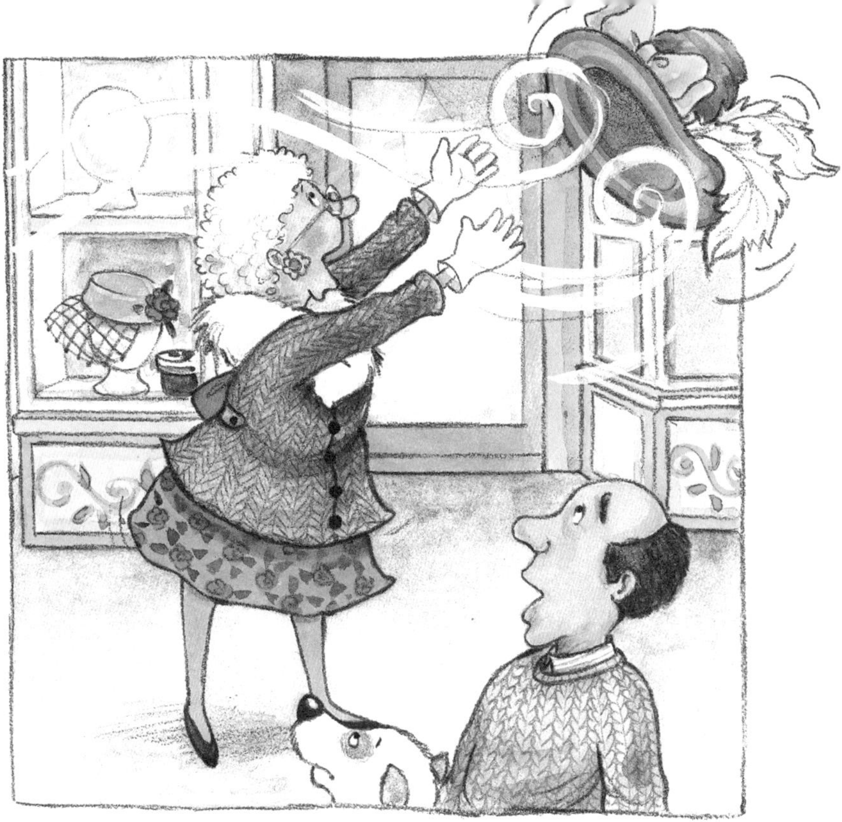

That is my pretty hat!

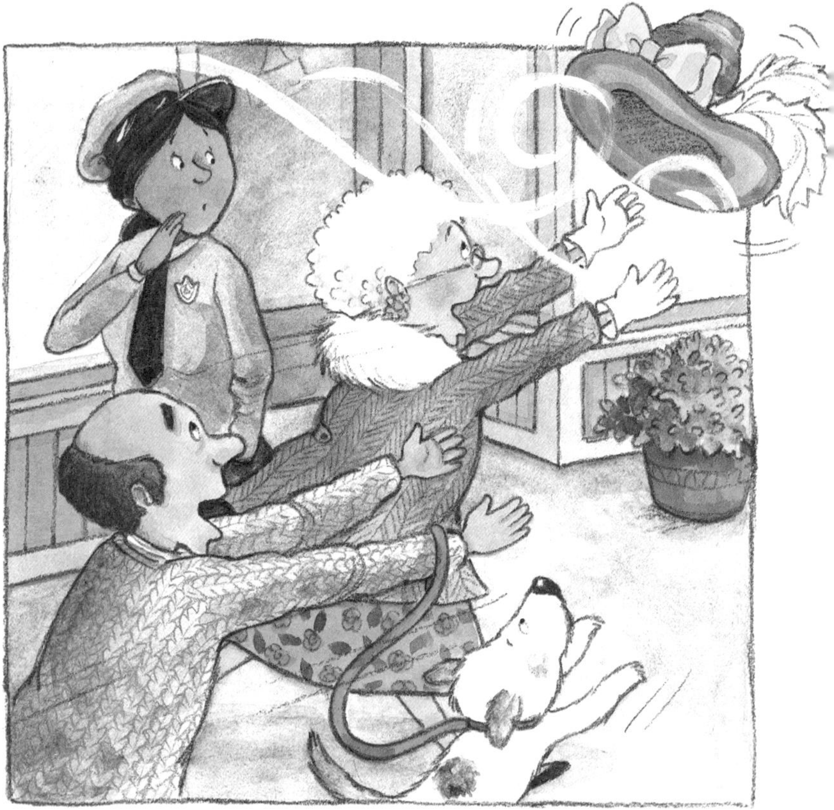

That is my pretty hat!

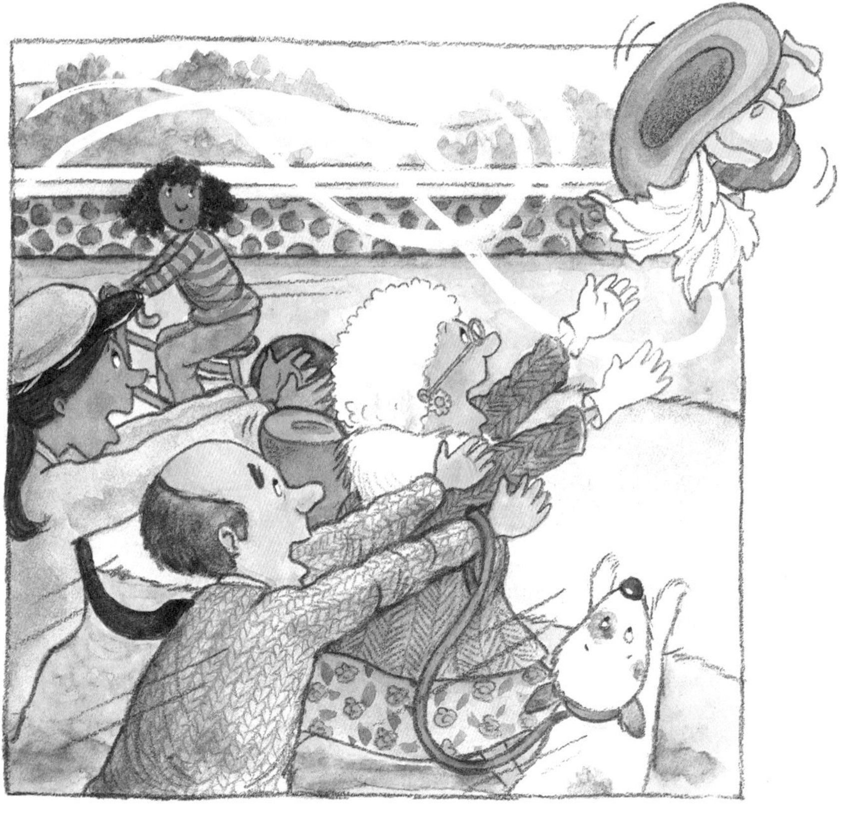

That is my pretty hat!

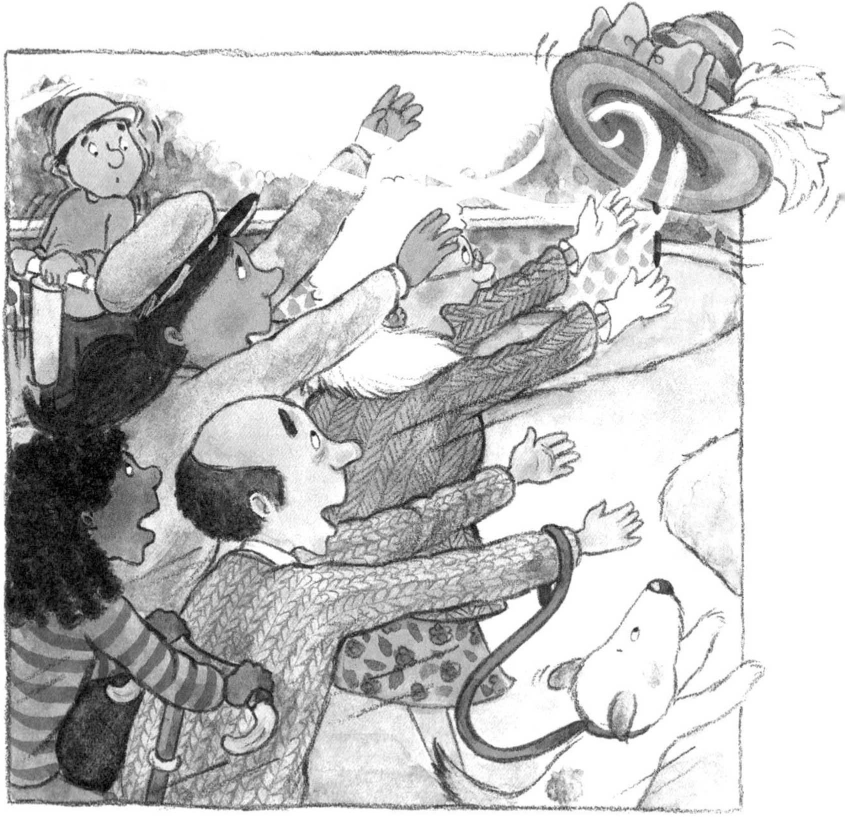

That is my pretty hat!

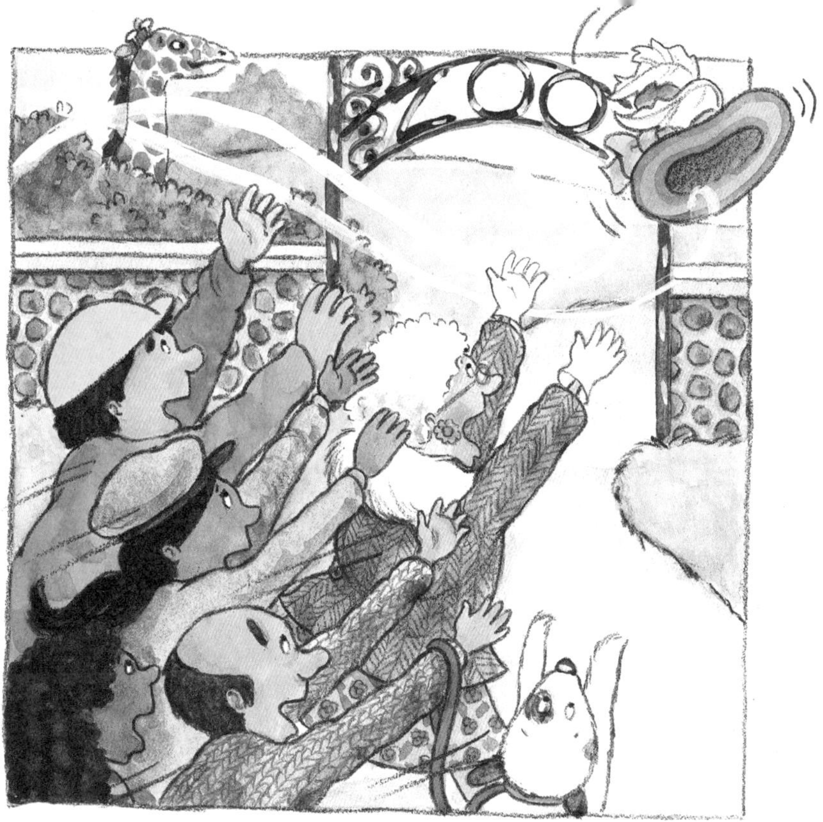

That is my pretty hat!

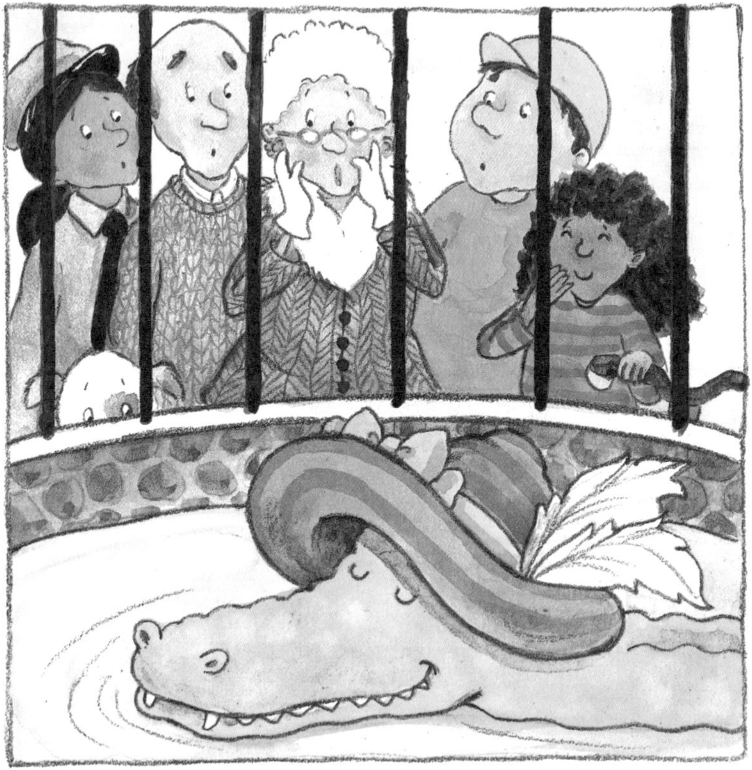

That is your pretty hat!